Because I Stubbed My Toe

by **shawn byous**

CAPSTONE YOUNG READERS
www.capstoneyoungreaders.com

BECAUSE I STUBBED MY TOE IS PUBLISHED BY CAPSTONE YOUNG READERS, A CAPSTONE IMPRINT
1710 ROE CREST DRIVE, NORTH MANKATO, MINNESOTA 56003
WWW.CAPSTONEYOUNGREADERS.COM

LIBRARY OF CONGRESS CATALOGING-IN-PUBLICATION DATA IS AVAILABLE ON THE LIBRARY OF CONGRESS WEBSITE.
ISBN: 978-1-62370-088-1 (HARDCOVER)
ISBN: 978-1-4795-3808-9 (PAPERBACK)

SUMMARY:
A YOUNG BOY STUBS HIS TOE, WHICH LEADS TO A SEQUENCE OF SILLY EVENTS AND A DELICIOUS ENDING.

DESIGNER:
RUSSELL JOHN GRIESMER

PRINTED IN THE UNITED STATES OF AMERICA IN NORTH MANKATO, MINNESOTA.
122013   007936

E
Byo

This morning I **stubbed** my toe.

And that **shook** the chair ...

which scared the dog ...

who **jumped** out the window ...

and landed on a girl ...
who **dropped** her ice-cream cone ...

causing a biker to **slide** off the road ...

and into a hive of bees ...

that **chased** an old man ...

who **jumped** into a pond ...

and **splashed** a surprised woman ...

who **tripped** and fell onto a teeter-totter ...

tossing a boy high into the air ...

who landed on a **crowded** bouncy house ...

which sent kids **running** and **screaming** ...

straight into the zoo ...

and scared the elephants ...

who **broke** out
of their cage ...

tromped down the street ...

knocked over an ice cream truck ...

and sent **loads** of ice cream
right through my window ...

Boy, am I glad I **stubbed** my toe!

The End